GUY the GRUMPY GARGOYLE

GILL JEPSON

Copyright © 2012 Gill Jepson

The moral right of the author has been asserted.

Matador
9 Priory Business Park
Kibworth Beauchamp
Leicestershire LE8 0RX, UK
Tel: (+44) 116 279 2299
Fax: (+44) 116 279 2277
Email: books@troubador.co.uk
Web: www.troubador.co.uk/matador

ISBN 978 1780882 222

British Library Cataloguing in Publication Data.
A catalogue record for this book is available from the British Library.

Typeset by Troubador Publishing Ltd, Leicester, UK

Matador is an imprint of Troubador Publishing Ltd

For Noah Jepson
And the children of Dalton St Mary's Primary school

Guy was a gargoyle. He lived at the top of a very high wall at Furness Abbey. He had many brothers all perched along the high walls around the church. He and his brothers were happy, looking down at the busy monks below, praying and working each day. He was proud to look over the abbey from his ledge, high above and watch the world go by.

At night, when the moon rose, something magical happened. He could stretch his bony arms, straighten his legs, unfold his wings and with a flick of his tail Guy was able to fly around the abbey and play with his brothers.

Time passed and things changed. Guy saw the king's soldiers knock down the walls and he shivered with fear. He watched as his brothers disappeared one by one. Some were brought down by the soldiers, some were taken away in carts to use in new buildings, others fell and broke into small pieces and some managed to hide away, but he never saw any of them again.

Guy was too frightened to move, he didn't want to disappear like his brothers. So, he stayed as still as the other stone statues in the abbey and was soon forgotten by everyone. He grew stiff and cold and refused to fly around the abbey when the moon was up. He settled into the ledge on the sandstone wall where he lived. He became grumpy and grouchy, his face growing more gruesome every day. He grew very, very old having lived there since the abbey was built many years ago.

He saw the plants and trees grow over the abbey and the sheep grazing on the grassy mounds where the buildings used to be. He watched the magpies nest in the walls and saw visitors come and go. He had nobody to talk to and nobody even knew he was still there.
Guy was lonely and sad.

The birds that nested nearby chirped at him and tried to cheer him up. Pretty white butterflies danced and played around his head trying to make him smile. Beautiful blue dragonflies fluttered and flickered in front of him trying to make him laugh...but nothing worked. Guy was lonely and sad.

His face grew grimmer and grumpier each day and he began growling and snarling at the creatures when they tried to make friends. The creatures became afraid of Guy because he was so bad tempered and rude. Guy didn't care; instead he became grumpier than ever.

Only one little creature dared to go near him and that was a tiny brown shrew, who lived in between the bricks in a small hole lined with soft, green moss. Selena the shrew was a kind little shrew. She felt sorry for Guy and understood how sad he was, because she missed her sisters since they had left the nest to make new homes in the woods.

Selena crept from her crack in the wall and crawled carefully up to where grumpy Guy sat.

"You can be happy Guy, if you try! All you need to do is smile and you will fly again," squeaked Selena.

"Humph!" grunted Guy.

She crept closer, crawling on to Guy's shoulder.

"Think of all the things there are to smile about: the beautiful birds, the delightful dragonflies and the brilliant butterflies, they're all your friends."

"Grrr," grumbled Guy.

Selena scurried along the curve of Guy's neck and up onto his nose. She sat firmly peering into his cross, little eyes. She wriggled her little tail and wrinkled her long, pointed nose, twitching her whiskers. Guy's nose quivered. Her tail tickled and teased and his nose trembled and wobbled. He could feel a sneeze growing and growing. Suddenly, he could hold it no longer…

"*A-aaa-choo*!" Guy sneezed, sending Selena scuttling up the wall to safety.

He could not help himself, he sneezed again,

"*A-aaa-choo*!" and again "*A-aaa-choo*!"

Finally, he started to smile, cracking the frown he had frozen onto his face for years. Small flakes of sandstone fell from his face, loosening his cheeks and his mouth.

Selena giggled, a squeaky, shrill, little laugh, which made Guy smile even wider. He sniggered and snorted, trying hard to stop the laughter from escaping, but it was no good. The little shrew had tickled him outside and in and he felt bubbles of chuckles rising from his tummy to his mouth, exploding with a huge cackle which echoed around the empty abbey.

"Ha-ha-ha-ha!"

He laughed so much that his sides hurt and his cheeks split into a happy grin. His eyes wrinkled with joy and tears of laughter ran down his sandstone cheeks, dissolving the grumpy frown completely.

The two of them made such a noise that the butterflies ventured nearer, the birds flew closer and the dragonflies hovered nearby. Soon the abbey rang with the laughter and chuckles of Guy and all the other animals.

The moon rose into the black, velvet sky and shone down on them, bathing everything in a silver light. Guy felt the light warm his skinny arms and his scrawny legs. He flexed his fingers and with a great effort wrenched himself away from the wall. He crouched nervously for a moment and unfolded his wings. He hesitated and everyone gasped as he prepared to fly. Selena scurried down and jumped onto his shoulder.

"Go on Guy! You can do it!" she squeaked.

He closed his eyes and hoped that he could still remember how to fly. With a great leap he launched himself from his stone ledge into the night air. He stretched his great wings wide and glided around the walls. The little shrew clung onto him, squealing with excitement.

They flew over the abbey, across the fields, through the trees and beyond the river. The birds, the butterflies and the dragonflies flew with them like a wonderful convoy of creatures. They flew through the night and into the dawn. As the sun broke through the clouds, the little gargoyle landed on his perch and settled back into position.

Guy smiled and his eyes closed, sending him into a happy contented sleep.

The next day, Guy woke up feeling lighter and happier than he had done for centuries. The sun shone, the bees buzzed and the birds sang. Selena was asleep on his feet. He was happy, until he thought about his brothers. He suddenly felt heavy and sad again. A big tear rolled down his cheek and fell PLOP onto Selena's head. She woke with a start.

"What's wrong Guy?" she piped.

"I miss my brothers!" sniffed Guy.

She tried to comfort him but he cried harder than ever.

Night fell and the silver moon rose high in the sky. Its silvery light melted the sadness away and Guy stretched and stood up on his ledge. Selena whispered in his big, pointed ear and a grin flashed across Guy's face.

The two of them flew down from the high wall and around the abbey ruins. They swooped down to the river and spotted a vole playing in the water. They landed close by and the vole jumped with surprise.

"Hello, young gargoyle. Can I help you?" he said.

"I'm looking for my brothers, do you know where they are?" asked Guy.

The vole looked at him with his little, black beady eyes and twitched his whiskers.

"Look like you, do they? he asked.

"Yes, *just* like me!" Guy replied.

The vole stroked his whiskers with his little paw.

"I don't think so," he said, "but if you go to the woods you can ask Owl, *he* knows everything."

Selena and Guy set off to the woods, flying into a clearing where a mighty oak stood. The old owl sat high in the hollow of the huge tree. He was just waking up and getting ready to go hunting for food.

"Hello young gargoyle, can I help you?" he boomed.

"Yes please Owl, I'm looking for my brothers, do you know where they are?"

Owl looked at him with his big, round, yellow eyes and fluttered his feathers.

"Look like you do they?"

"Yes, *just* like me!" Guy replied.

He turned his head to the left and then to the right.

"I don't think so," he said, "but if you go down to the field you can ask Badger, *he* knows everything."

They raced through the wood and down to the field, to the sett where Badger lived. He too had just woken up and was getting ready to go hunting for food.

"Hello young gargoyle, can I help you?" he rumbled.

"Yes please Badger, I'm looking for my brothers, do you know where they are?"

Badger looked at him with his little black eyes and scratched his fur.

"Look like you do they?"

"Yes, *just* like me!" Guy replied.

He stuck his long snout in the air and sniffed.

"I don't think so," he said, "but if you go down to the pond you can ask Swan, *she* knows everything."

They set off through the field to the pond where Swan lived. She was asleep with her head tucked under her wing. She woke and lifted her head when they landed on the bank.

"Hello young gargoyle, can I help you?" she whispered gently.

"Yes, please Swan, I'm looking for my brothers, do you know where they are?"

Swan looked at him with her little, black eyes and flapped her beautiful, white wings.

"Look like you, do they?"

"Yes, *just* like me!" Guy replied.

She stretched her long neck and then flexed her beautiful wings.

"Yes I think so," she said, "if you go down to the Abbey Mill Café, you will find one of your brothers in the garden. He looks *just* like you and is very lonely."

Selena and Guy were excited. They flew over the pond, across the field, through the woods, along the river and over the cottage where the café was. Guy swooped down, over the roof and landed on the grass.

There were some statues in the garden, among the flowers and the grass. Right in the centre of a flower bed sat… a grumpy, grouchy gargoyle, *just* like Guy!

Guy flapped his wings and swished his tail excitedly.

"Gregory!" he cried, "Is that you? My brother?"

The grisly, grim little gargoyle looked up, his sandstone face cracked and splintered with a huge smile as he recognised his brother.

The two gargoyles danced and jumped for glee. They laughed and cried, hugged and kissed. They were happy again.

Selena scuttled in between them, running over their clawed feet and round their scrawny legs.

The three friends danced the night away and when they were tired, they flew up to the top of the abbey and rested on the empty ledges high above the ground. The little shrew crept back into her nest and fell into a happy sleep. Guy and Gregory slept too.

So now, instead of being grumpy gargoyles, Guy and Gregory, were jolly gargoyles who smiled down at all the visitors during the day and flew around the abbey by night.